THE SIMPLE
GIFT

steven herrick

Simon Pulse
New York London Toronto Sydney

**to my dad, in memory,
to my mum, who always
welcomed me back.**

First Simon Pulse edition May 2004

Copyright © 2000 by Steven Herrick
Originally published in Australia in 2000 by University of Queensland Press
Published by arrangement with University of Queensland Press

SIMON PULSE
An imprint of Simon & Schuster
Children's Publishing Division
1230 Avenue of the Americas
New York, NY 10020

Designed by Ann Sullivan
The text of this book was set in Jansen.

Printed in the United States of America
10 9 8 7 6 5 4 3 2 1

Library of Congress Control Number 2003110837
ISBN 0-689-86867-7

Contents

1
Champagne Billy

*"I say goodbye to all that,
throwing rocks down Longlands Road."*

Champagne

Billy

It's the only time my schoolbag
has come in handy.
I tip my books, pens, jumper
out on my bed,
shake yesterday's sandwich, squashed,
from the bottom of the bag.
I go to the kitchen,
take the beer,
last night's leftovers,
some glossy red apples,
Dad's champagne and cigarettes,
load my schoolbag,
my travelling bag,
leave the bottle of lemonade on the table
with a note,

    "See ya Dad.
    I've taken the alcohol.
    Drink this instead
    to celebrate your son
    leaving home."

The old bastard will have a fit!
And me?
I'll be long gone.

Kiss the dog

Billy

I'm not proud.
I'm sixteen, and soon
to be homeless.
I sit on the veranda
and watch the cold rain fall.
Bunkbrain, our dog,
sits beside me.
I'd like to take him with me.
He doesn't deserve to stay
in this dump, no-one does.
But you don't get rides
with a dog.
And two mouths to feed
is one too many.
Bunkbrain knows something,
he nuzzles in close,
his nose wet and dirty
from sniffing for long-lost bones.
I scratch behind his ears
and kiss the soft hair
on his head.
I'll miss you dog.
I'm not proud.
I'm leaving.
The rain falls steady.
Bunkbrain stays on the veranda.

Longlands Road

Billy

This place has never looked
so rundown and beat.
Old Basten's truck still on blocks,
the grass unmown around the doors.
Mrs Johnston's mailbox on the ground
after I took to it with a cricket bat
last week.
And the windows to the Spencer house
still broken
from New Year's Eve,
it must get cold in the front room
at night.
My street.
My suburb.
I take a handful of rocks,
golf ball size.
I walk slowly in the rain
the bag on my back.
I throw one rock on the roof
of each deadbeat no-hoper
shithole lonely downtrodden house
in Longlands Road, Nowheresville.
The rocks bounce and clatter
and roll and protest
at being left in this damn place.
I say goodbye to all that,
throwing rocks down Longlands Road.

Wentworth High School Billy

I reach school at 4:30
in the rainy afternoon
of my goodbyes.
Principal Viera's Holden
pulls out of the car park
and blows smoke down the road.
I jump the fence
and walk the grounds.
The wind howls and rain sheets in
blowing potato crisp wrappers
across the oval.
I go to Room 421
and look through the window.
Mr Cheetam's homework is on the board.
26 students are learning
about the geography of Japan
and one lucky bastard is writing
"may you all get
well and truly stuffed"
on the window
in K-Mart Red lipstick
stolen especially for this occasion.
I sign my name in red
"Billy Luckett,
rhymes with . . ."
Let Cheetam chew on that.

Westfield Creek

Billy

I love this place.
I love the flow of cold clear water
over the rocks
and the wattles on the bank
and the lizards sunbaking,
heads up, listening,
and the birds,
hundreds of them,
silver-eyes and currawongs,
kookaburras laughing
at us kids swinging on the rope
and dropping into the bracing flow.
I spent half my school days here
reading books I'd stolen
from Megalong Bookshop
with old Tom Whitton
thinking I'm his best customer
buying one book
with three others shoved up my jumper.
I failed every Year Eleven subject
except English.
I can read.
I can dream.
I know about the world.
I learnt all I need to know
in books on the banks
of Westfield Creek,
my favourite classroom.

Please

The Great Western Highway
is not much of a highway,
not great at all,
but it does head west,
which is where I'm going
if one of these damn cars
will only stop and give me a ride.
Two hours in the dark
in the rain
in the dirt of this bloody road
is not getting me anywhere.
What to do?
Go home?
    "Say Dad,
    I still want to leave
    but I couldn't get a lift
    so one more night
    that's OK with you, isn't it?"
He'd be sober because I stole
    his beer
    his champagne.
No. I can't go back.
I could sleep at school,
on the veranda.
One more hour of this,
just one ride,
please.

Freight train Billy

Not one car has passed
in the last twenty minutes.
At least the rain has stopped.
I'm sitting on my bag
looking across at the freight train
stopped at the crossing
for no good reason.
Fifty coal carriages,
empty,
heading to the Waggawang Coalfields
and one carriage
with a speedboat strapped on top.
A speedboat on a train
heading west?
To what?
A coalfield lake?
The inland river system
dry as a dead dingo's bones?
And then it hits me.
Who cares. It's heading west,
and I'm not . . .
so . . .
I race across the highway,
bag swinging,
and the train whistle blows
as I reach the bushes beside the track,
a quick glance, both ways,
and I'm up on the carriage
pulling myself into the

Aquadream Speedboat
with the soft padded bench seat,
the Evinrude outboard motor
and the fishing gear.
The train whistle blows again
and we lurch forward
as I get my ride
on a speedboat out of town
and not a lake for miles.

Cold   Billy

Two kilometres down the track
I realise
how fast trains go
when you've got no window to close
and the wind and rain
hits you in the face
with the force of a father's punch.
I unpack my bag
put my jacket on
wrap a jumper around my ears and neck
put my spare pants on
over my trousers
and I'm still freezing
and the whistle keeps blowing
as we speed through the bitter night.
I'll be frozen dead
before morning.
I snuggle under the bow
of this speeding speedboat
cutting the night
my knees tight against my chest
and my teeth clenched
in some wild frost-bitten grin
and that train whistle keeps me sane
blowing across every dirt road crossing
with flashing red lights
and not a soul awake
except the train driver

warm in his cabin
and the idiot
hunched under the bow
praying for morning and sunshine.

Keep warm Ernie

"Hey kid,
get outta there.
You'll freeze to death.
That'll teach you
to hitch a ride with National Rail.
No free rides with this government, son.
Just kidding.
I hate the bloody government.
Get your bag
and come back to the Guard's van.
There's a heater that works,
and some coffee.
We've stopped here
waiting for the Interstate.
Passengers snoring in their comfy cabins
get priority
over empty coal trains.
Say, what do you think of me boat?
Yep, mine.
I got a special deal to bring it home.
We've got a lake outside of town,
perfect for fishing
and getting away from the telly.
I'm going to sit in this tub
and drink myself stupid
every weekend.
There you go.
Make a cuppa if you want.
And here's some sandwiches,

too much salad for my liking.
Just don't tell anyone about this, OK.
I'll see you in the morning.
We'll be in Bendarat at dawn.
I'll blow the whistle three times
and I'll stop just before town.
Jump out then, OK.

Keep warm.
I've got a train to drive."

Men

There are men like Ernie,
the train driver, in this world.
Men who don't boss you around
and don't ask prying questions
and don't get bitter
at anyone different from them.
Men who share a drink and food
and a warm cabin
when they don't have to.
Men who know the value of things
like an old boat
built for long weekends on a lake.
Men who see something happening
and know if it's right
or wrong
and aren't afraid to make that call.
There are men like Ernie
and
there are other men,
men like my dad.

Sport

Billy

I was ten years old
in the backyard
kicking a soccer ball
against the bedroom wall,
practising for the weekend.
My first season of sport
and I'd already scored a goal,
so I kept practising, alone.
And I guess I tried too hard,
I kicked it too high,
stupid of me I know,
and I broke the bedroom window.
I stood in the yard
holding the ball
looking at the crack in the pane.
Dad came thundering out.
He didn't look at the damage.
He'd heard it.
He grabbed the ball,
kicked it over the back fence
into the bush,
gave me one hard backhander
across the face,
so hard I fell down
as much in shock as anything,
and I felt the blood
from my nose,
I could taste it dribbling out
as Dad stood over me

and said
no more sport
no more forever.
He walked back inside
and slammed the door
on my sporting childhood
that disappeared into the bush
with my soccer ball.

I was ten years old.
I didn't go inside for hours.
I looked through the back window
watching him
reading the paper
in front of the television
as if nothing
had happened.

Another crossing

Billy

Ernie was right,
too much salad in the sandwich,
but I ate it all the same.
I had a coffee
heaped with sugar
sweet and hot
and I felt warm
like Ernie had wished.
I took the champagne
out of my bag
and stood it on the table
between Ernie's coffee pot
and his lunchbox.
I wrote a note.
     "Thanks Ernie.
     Here's a present
     to launch your boat.
     Don't smash it though!
     Drink it."
I heard the whistle again
and looked out at
another lonesome crossing
and felt glad
that the champagne
was going to someone
who deserved it.

2
Bendarat

"I'd go off alone,
because you can't trust
those who want to break the rules
and you certainly can't trust
those who make the rules,
so you do the only thing possible,
you avoid the rules."

Bendarat

Billy

Dawn is fog-closed and cold.
A ute bounces along the dirt road
beside the track,
its lights dancing in the mist.
I see a street sign,
"Bendarat—5 kilometres."
I pack my bag quickly,
warm my hands
close to the heater
and wait for the three whistles
to dump me in another State,
miles from home
miles from school,
with the sun finally
lifting the fog
as the train slows
and Ernie whistles good luck.
I climb down,
wave ahead,
and walk slowly
into Bendarat.

Tonight, and the night after

Billy

The walk stretches my cold body.
As I near town there's more cars
and school buses, yellow,
full of kids shouting insults
at me, the bum,
walking down the road.
I don't care,
better a bum than a school kid.
It's an old town
with stone buildings
and wide streets
and cast-iron street lamps
like crazy ghosts lurking
on the footpaths.
And every shop has a SALE sign
like the whole town's
desperate for money.
As I walk down Main Street
thinking of the $50 in my pocket
and how it's got to last me
a lifetime
I realise Bendarat
is not the only desperate one.
But, today
I don't care.
The sun is shining now
as I reach the library
and sit down on the front steps,
one hour until opening.

My day today is reading,
reading about people who don't need money
and people
who have somewhere to sleep
tonight,
and the night after.

Lord of the lounge   Billy

It's a good library.
Lots of books, sure,
and lounges soft and comfortable
for real reading,
and I choose one
in the corner
and I settle down
with a book about these kids
stranded on a deserted island
and some try to live right
but the others go feral
and it's a good book
and I'm there, on the island,
gorging on tropical fruit,
trying to decide
whose side I'm on.
And then it hits me.
I'm on neither.
I'd go off alone,
because you can't trust
those who want to break the rules
and you certainly can't trust
those who make the rules,
so you do the only thing possible,
you avoid the rules.
That's me,
on the deserted island
of a soft lounge
in Bendarat Library.

The librarian

"You can borrow that if you like."

Her badge says
Irene Thompson—Chief Librarian.
Trouble I'm sure.

"It's a good book.
It was my favourite when I was young."

"No thanks.
I'm happy to read it here."
Please just leave me alone.
"That's fine.
But we close for lunch in ten minutes.
I'm sorry. But you can come back at 2."

"Thanks Mrs Thompson. I will.
It's too good a book not to finish."
She's OK.
Not like the librarian at home.
She hated kids touching books.
She ran the perfect library
because no-one ever went in there
to disturb the books.

"Call me Irene.
I'm old, but not that old.
See you after lunch."

Lunch

Billy

I'm poor, homeless,
but I'm not stupid.
For lunch I go to Coles.
I buy a packet of bread rolls,
some cheese and a tomato.
Enough for three meals.
I sit on the bench
at Bendarat Gardens
with my Swiss Army Knife
cutting thin slices of tomato
with chunks of cheese
and I eat two rolls
watching the pigeons
watching me.
I toss them some crumbs.
Lunchtime entertainment,
free of charge,
is a couple kissing on a blanket.
For twenty minutes
they lay together
kissing
hugging.
They hardly touch their sandwiches.
I can't blame them.
As they get up to leave
I feel like applauding,
but as I said
I'm poor, homeless,
but I'm not stupid.

The Motel Bendarat   Billy

I finish the book,
nod goodbye to Irene
and walk out
into the late afternoon cloud
and a slight drizzle.
No sleeping in the park tonight.
Two options:
a church
or a railway station.
Churches are too spooky and cold.
I walk to the station.
Men in suits, like tired penguins,
wait for the bus
and throw furtive glances
at the woman on the seat
reading a magazine.
She ignores them.

The train station is sandstone
with a long veranda platform,
hard wooden seats and a Coke machine.
I walk across the tracks
past the Freight Yard
to some old carriages,
disused, waiting to be sold
and turned into
fancy Bed & Breakfast Accommodation
or maybe used as someone's chookshed.
I try each door until one opens.

I climb in.
There's a long bench seat
fit to hold eight people
and certainly long enough
for me to sleep on.
It's comfortable too,
being old and well made.
I close the door
and make a home
in Carriage 1864,
painted red and yellow,
my Motel Bendarat.

Night

Billy

I have two rolls for dinner,
washed down with
the last of Dad's beer.
The carriage is surprisingly warm
and quiet, so quiet.
I use my bag as a pillow,
wrap my jacket over me,
lay back and sleep
the sleep of the dreamless.
Occasionally I wake
to a train whistle
or the clank of metal on metal
as the night shift works,
shunting the freight carriages.
I think of Bunkbrain, my dog,
probably asleep on the veranda
and I wish I'd brought him
for the company
on nights like this
in a new town
and in a new home.

Eating out

Billy

I finished the rolls
and cheese for lunch today,
so tonight I'm eating out.
McDonald's.
I order a small lemonade,
no ice,
no fries,
no burger,
and no smile from the lady
behind the counter.
She's the Manager I'm sure.
Everyone else working here is my age
except this lady
who looks at me as if I'm diseased
for ordering only a drink.
I go upstairs
where it's quiet and warm.
I read the free newspaper
and wait.
Sure enough
the couple in the corner
can't eat all the fries,
and the woman leaves half a burger.
They get up to leave
and before they've reached the stairs
I'm over at the table,
grabbing the burger
and the fries
to go with my lemonade,

the lemonade I bought.
This is the only way to eat at McDonald's.
I sit back
read the newspaper
and wait for the family of five to leave.
I can see dessert
waiting for me.

3
Caitlin

*"As if we were both caught
doing something
we didn't want to do
but had to."*

Caitlin and mopping

When I first saw what he did
I wanted to go up
and say,
"Put that food back."
But how stupid is that?
It was going in the rubbish
until he claimed it.
So I watched him.
He was very calm.
He didn't look worried
about being caught
or ashamed of stealing scraps.
He looked relaxed,
as though he knew he had to eat
and this was the easiest way.
I had work to do,
mopping the floor,
which I hate,
so I mopped slowly
and watched.
He read the paper
until the family left,
then he helped himself to dessert,
and as he walked back to his table,
holding the apple pie,
he looked up and saw me
watching him.
He stood over his table
waiting for me to do something.

He stood there
almost daring me to get the Manager,
who I hate
almost as much as I hate mopping.
So I smiled at him.
I smiled and said,
"I hate mopping."
He sat in his chair
and smiled back
and I felt good
that I hadn't called the Manager.
I kept mopping.
He finished his dessert,
came over to me,
looked at my badge,
looked straight at me,
and said, "Goodnight, Caitlin,"
and he walked out,
slow and steady,
and so calm,
so calm.

Too rich

Caitlin

I don't need to work at McDonald's.
Dad would rather I didn't.
He buys me anything I want.
But Mum and I have a deal.
Whatever I earn she doubles
and banks for me,
for university in two years.
Dad says why bother.
Dad is too rich for his own good.
It was his idea I go to
Bendarat Grammar School
instead of Bendarat High School
where all my old friends went.
So I wear the tartan skirt
and the clean white blouse
and I shine my shoes every week
and wear the School Blazer on Sports Day,
and feel like a real dork
when I see my old friends
in the street in jeans and T-shirts.
Bendarat High
has a "progressive uniform policy"
which means "wear what you like,"
while Grammar
is Discipline and Charity and Honesty
and all those other words
schools like to put on their Crests
so they can charge people like my dad
$10,000 a year

to make me wear a uniform.
and I can't wait for university
so I can leave home
and that's why I work at McDonald's
and mop floors.

Billy

She had clean hair.
Bouncing, shiny, clean hair.
That's the first thing I noticed.
And her skin was pale and clear
and I knew she was rich
because I saw her watch
and it shone like her hair.
Her eyes were pale green
and they seemed to know
something I didn't,
they seemed to be thinking.
Can eyes think?
And when I saw her watching me
take the food
my first thought was to hate her
because of that shiny watch
and her perfect skin
and I knew she'd call the Manager
and I'd be out of there,
but she just smiled
and complained about the mopping
as if we were both caught
doing something
we didn't want to do
but had to.

Breakfast

Billy

Bendarat is the perfect town.
A friendly librarian,
a warm McDonald's,
luxury train accommodation,
and the town is surrounded by
apple and pear orchards.
So every morning
I walk the two kilometres
to the Golden Crest Cannery Farm.
I climb the fence
and help myself to a
healthy breakfast of fruit.
Then I walk slowly
back to town,
past the Bendarat Grammar School.
Yes, I bet Caitlin goes there.
I cross the road.
I wouldn't want to meet her here
not when she's with her friends
and in uniform
and me
dressed in the same clothes as always.
All the students look clean
and rich and smug
and confident,
and I thought of Caitlin
and decided I shouldn't judge,
not yet anyway.

Hunger

Caitlin

Now I'm not going to admit
to liking the work at McDonald's,
particularly mopping,
but since he arrived
it's certainly more interesting.
Tonight he did the usual,
cleaned the tables,
ate his fill,
sipped his lemonade,
and said, "Goodnight, Caitlin,"
but when I went to
clean his table
I found a note
that read
"Did you know that
Caitlin is an Irish name
from Catherine
meaning pure and innocent?"

I read this and felt
something in my stomach,
a slight ache, a twinge,
and I knew it was hunger
but not a hunger for food.

Manners

Caitlin

He came back tonight,
sat in the same chair,
and waited.
I mopped, as usual,
and watched him.
Tonight was busier.
He had lots to choose from.
He ate slowly.
We each nodded hello.
The Manager came upstairs
so I couldn't say anything.
When she left
I mopped over near his table.
He said, "Hello, Caitlin,"
as if we were friends,
so I stopped mopping,
stood straight
and said, "I'm Caitlin Holmes."
He stood and shook my hand
and replied, "Billy Luckett."
Such perfect manners,
eating scraps at McDonald's.

Business

This time when he left
he came over to me
and he had something
in his hand.
It was a business card.
He gave it to me
and said,
"Goodnight, Caitlin."
So well-mannered,
so unlike every boy
at Bendarat Grammar,
or any schoolboy I've ever known.
I looked at the card.

> Peter Robinson
> Electrical Contractor
> Farley St Bendarat.
> Lic# G254378

It didn't make sense.

Then I turned it over.

> Bill Luckett
> Unemployed
> Carriage 1864
> Bendarat Freight Yard
> No Licence/No Certificate.

I smiled to myself.
Homeless, and proud of it.

Caitlin

Caitlin

I'm a normal seventeen-year-old girl.
I think about boys.
I sit with my girlfriends, Kate and Petra,
at lunchtime.
Sometimes we talk to boys
when they sit with us.
I watch Petra flirt madly
and I notice her body language
change when boys are near.
She moves her hands more,
her eyes wink and flutter,
she's such a show pony,
but I like her.
And I've been out with boys
"on dates"
but mostly with Petra and Kate
and a whole gang together,
not alone.
And I've done some things,
you know,
at parties with boys,
just mild stuff really.
So I'm normal,
a normal seventeen-year-old.
I think about boys
but only in a general way
like not a boy I know
or anything
but just some good-looking guy

and me
and what we'd do
if we had the chance.
Pure fantasy really.
Nothing wrong with that,
but nothing real about it either.

4
The hobo hour

"Every second day
I come here . . .
to wash the world away."

The hobo hour

Billy

It's morning
but still dark
when I hear a bottle crash
outside the carriage.
I go out to check
and find
an old man
with long grey hair
and beard
sitting on the train track
looking at the beer stain
the wooden sleepers.
He can't believe he's dropped
a full bottle.
He sits there, staring,
doesn't notice me
behind him.
I don't know whether
to leave him be
or say sorry
although I didn't do anything.
Then I remember
Dad's carton of cigarettes
in my bag.
I don't smoke.
I just stole them
to annoy Dad.
I rush back into the carriage
and get them.

I sit beside the old hobo
and hand them across.
He looks at them awhile,
then at me,
smiles weakly,
takes them, saying,
"I should give up.
These will kill me."
He unwraps the carton,
hands shaking,
lights one
and takes a huge drag.
The tip of the cigarette
burns brightly
then
fades to old smoke.
We both sit
staring at the beer
and the sunrise,
sharing the hobo hour.

Old Bill

His name,
would you believe,
is Bill.
So I decided to call him
Old Bill.
He didn't mind.
He said he'd slept
in the carriage next to mine
on and off
for years.
He'd bought himself
a bottle of beer
to celebrate his birthday,
and look at it now.
His grey beard was stained with smoke,
his hair long and swept back,
his face lined but
when you looked closer
he wasn't that old,
forty-five, maybe fifty.
He got up to go to bed
to sleep off his sorrow
or so he said.
As he left he turned
and said,
"Welcome to the Bendarat Hilton,
I've been here since March 2nd, 1994.
May your stay be as long,
if you wish it."

Then he stumbled off,
an old man
before his time,
sleeping in a carriage,
and I shivered
as the sun came up.

Rich town

Billy

In the late afternoon
Old Bill told me
that Bendarat was once
the railway hub of the south-west.
A rich town,
with pubs on every corner
and drunken railway workers
walking the streets looking for action.
Over one hundred men
worked in the Freight Yard
on eight-hour shifts
around the clock,
loading cross-country trains
with wheat and wool
and fruit from the orchards.
A rich town.

But the highways improved
and semitrailers were faster than trains
and they built a wheat silo
outside of town
so now
there's only a few men left
driving forklifts
loading fruit pallets
and that's all.

Old Bill said
the workers

know he's here
but they don't say anything
to the authorities
because
he keeps the carriage clean
and doesn't make much noise
and, like the few workers left,
he's got nowhere else to go
and nothing else to do,
in Bendarat,
that once
was a rich town.

Before my time

Billy

I slept badly.
I dreamt of myself
as an old man
in a pub, at the bar,
watching the races on TV
with my smokes and my plans
for winning $5 on the grey horse
running second last.
All night
I could hear Old Bill
snoring, coughing,
swearing in his sleep.
He made more noise
than the wind
whistling through the Freight Yard.
I lay in bed
listening
afraid to fall asleep
and dream again
of myself
getting old
long before my time.

Too early   Billy

This morning,
too early,
I get a bowl
and fill it with Weet-Bix and milk
and I take it next door
to Old Bill.
I knock quietly
and I hear him grunt.
I open the door
to his carriage,
to the smell of old socks
and alcohol
mixed with the Weet-Bix,
the Weet-Bix I offer
to Old Bill
as I lean inside.
He lifts his head slightly,
shields his eyes
from the light,
and he growls,
"Piss off, son.
Piss off. Leave me alone."
It's too early
for a drunk,
too early for most of us I guess.
I leave the bowl and a spoon
and I close the door
and walk away
into the fragile morning.

Bendarat River

Billy

The river is cold, clear,
and deep. Outside of town
there's a weir where the water
falls swiftly over rocks
and forms whirlpools
and bubbles and makes more noise
than the cockatoos in the river gums.
Further downstream it rounds a slow bend
and here I swim fully-clothed
and stand waist-deep in the shallows
with a bar of soap.
I wash my clothes and myself
in one soapy afternoon
swim in the deep,
feel the weight of my clothes
pulling me down
but I'm a strong swimmer.
I reach the bank
and undress to my Speedos
and hang my pants, shirt,
and sweater in the trees
to dry.
Every second day
I come here
to the Bendarat Laundry
to wash the world away.

Old Bill

Old Bill

I guess I shouldn't be surprised
by anything anymore.
The kid must be fifteen,
or sixteen at the most,
and here he is,
living at the Bendarat Hilton
with a bag of clothes
and some smokes
to give away
to a bum like me.
And when he gave me
those smokes
I almost cried,
a kid like that
with nothing
giving stuff away.
But I took them
and I sat in my carriage
smoking
and trying to place
the past five years
and my memory
flickered and grew dim
like the cigarette
and I stopped remembering
because I knew
where my thoughts
would take me.
And the cigarette

tasted foul
and I flicked
the butt out the window.
It died on the tracks
quickly
in the cold night air
of a bum's
stumbling memory.

Caitlin visiting

I finish work every night at 9.
Dad always waits up for me.
But tonight I tell Dad
I'm going to Petra's to study
and I make Petra promise
to sit by the phone
should my parents ring
and if they ring
she's to tell them
I'm in the bathroom
and I'll call back.
Then she's to ring me
on my mobile and I'll
ring them and no-one
will know where I am.
Sometimes being rich
and having a dad who
spoils you and buys you
completely stupid
unnecessary crap like
a gold watch
and a mobile phone
has its advantages.
After work
I change into jeans and
a heavy wool jumper
and my long overcoat
and into my schoolbag
I place two apple pies

and I ask the Manager
for two cups of coffee,
to go.
My dad always said
that you should take
something, a gift,
when you go visiting.

Billy's cave

Caitlin

I'm well-mannered.
I knock on the door
of Carriage 1864 and wait.
I knock again.
Then I hear his voice
behind me.
I almost drop the coffee
and he apologises for scaring me.
He takes the coffee
and we go inside.
There are two long leather seats
facing each other.
On one he's stacked books
and clothes and bits & pieces
of things he's found,
like old bottles and a tin drum.
On the other lay his sleeping bag
and his rucksack as a pillow.
It's clean and warm.
He shows me the broom
and the kerosene heater
he's found.
It's like a little cave,
a warm, safe little cave
for children to hide in
when
they're scared or lonely
and need somewhere safe
to go.
Billy's cave.

Picnic

Billy

I hear the knock and jump.
Cops? Railway Security?
I crawl out the back window,
drop quietly onto the track
and skirt along the carriage.
Then I realise cops or security
wouldn't knock!
They'd come barging in
looking for a fight.
So I come in from behind
and see who it is.
I swallow hard,
now I am nervous.
I say hello
and she jumps.
Great start.
I invite her into my carriage,
and watch her as she
sees how I live.
She's cool.
She doesn't sneer or
look uncomfortable.
She sits on the seat
and puts her feet up
as though she belongs.
I sit opposite
and we drink coffee,
eat apple pie,
and feel like two kids
on a picnic.

Looking

Billy

I tell Caitlin
about leaving home,
the champagne,
and Ernie,
and my days spent
in the library reading books
and researching the meaning of names
like Caitlin,
and Luckett,
which is Scottish in origin.
I found an ancestor
who was a Duke—
from royalty to unemployment
in a few generations.
Something to be proud of.
I'm nervous
but I keep talking.
She listens
and smiles
and her eyes
never stray from me,
but the more she looks at me
the more relaxed I become
and I look back
and I see past
the shiny watch
and the clean hair
and the beautiful woollen overcoat.
I like what I see.

Happen

Caitlin

I tell Petra
about Billy and my visit.
I tell her about his cave
and his library days
and how he reads more
and knows more
than anybody I've met
and as I talk
the thought comes,
"What now?"
And Petra reads my mind.
"What now?" she says.
I look at her,
at the school
with its stone tower
and huge clock
and teachers dressed in suits
and the Indoor Sports Centre
with its heated pool,
and the rose garden
skirting the circular driveway.
The lunch bell sounds.
Petra and I stand
and I say,
"I'll visit him again,
and again,
until something happens."

And all next period
I think of what could happen
and what
I could want to happen.

Going nowhere

Billy

I sleep well,
warm in the railway dark,
the mail train whistle
and the town hall clock
sounding the hours.
This morning I wake
and I know where I'm going
for the next few months—
to the Library
to McDonald's
to the river
and home here to the Hilton—
a circuit of plans
with Caitlin at the centre,
and me
a badly-dressed satellite
spinning crazily in her orbit.

**5
Work**

*"A kid
who can't leave well enough
alone."*

Sorry

Old Bill

I feel sorry
for swearing at the kid,
abusing him for bringing me breakfast.
Breakfast! Of all things.
A good kid,
living like a bum
and I knew he'd need money,
even bums need money to live.
So this morning, early,
far too bloody early for me,
I knock on his door
to return the bowl and spoon
and he opens it slowly,
invites me in,
and I tell him
about the Cannery and work.
How every Monday during the season
they offer work,
and if he needs money
that's the place to go,
and he says,
"Sure, great. Let's go."
And because I'm still sorry
about swearing at him
I find myself
walking to the Cannery
with the kid
looking for work,

work I don't need,
or want.
Walking with the kid
early Monday morning.

Work

7:30 Monday morning.
Old Bill and me
at the gates of the
Golden Crest Cannery
with six other men
waiting
for the foreman
who saunters out
points at two blokes
then me and Old Bill
and tells us to follow him.
We do. We need to.
He takes us into the Cannery,
the noise, the smell
overpowers everything
but my need for money.
He leaves Old Bill and me
on the tomato line.
A conveyor belt
of overripe fruit
circles the cutting table
where we stand
with apron and gloves,
a hairnet and a knife.
The head lady
shows us what to do—
cut only the black fetid bits
from the fruit
put the overripe mess

back on the belt
where it heads to the crusher
for soup
and sauce
and somebody's kitchen table—
while I
pick and cut and slice
and think only
of the $12 an hour cash,
waiting at the end of the week.

That bloody kid

Old Bill

Every morning this week
that bloody kid
has woken me at 6:30
with Weet-Bix and milk
and the thought of another day
cutting up pieces of overripe fruit.
This is what I get
for feeling sorry.

I tell him to piss off, again,
but he ignores me now.
He thinks I need the money,
or the company,
or the early mornings,
when what I really need
is to be left alone.
Bloody hell.
Work.
I haven't worked in years.
I haven't done anything in years.
Look at me,
walking along beside the kid
to the Cannery.
And he never shuts up,
he talks about this girl he's met
and how friendly she is
and I've half a mind to tell him
to get her to go to work with him
and leave me alone,

but he prattles on
until we reach the Cannery
and another day of rotten fruit.
But at least
I'm not drinking so much,
and I can't smoke in the Cannery.
Bloody hell,
this kid's going to turn me
into a health freak!

My hands

Billy

At the end of three days work
my hands are stained red
and smell of rotten tomatoes
and every night
at McDonald's
waiting for the leftovers
I pray the burgers
are without sauce
and I can't eat the fries
splashed with blood-thick liquid.
I know where it comes from,
not fresh from the orchard
with a handsome farmer
holding up firm shiny ripe fruit.
I know it comes from a conveyor belt
where coughing workers
cut the mould
and the black growth
from squashed red mush,
and I remember the fingernails
of the workers
and I hope the gloves were tight
and disease-proof
as I watch families pass the
sauce packets
from sister to brother,
and I look at my hands,
the hands of a worker
tomato red and raw.

Burning

Billy

I sign the form
and the lady hands me
the yellow envelope.
I walk out into
afternoon sunshine
and sit on the bench
with Old Bill.
I count the notes
5 days—38 hours
$456 minus tax
and I'm left with
more money than
I've ever had in my life.
I ask Old Bill
what he's going to do with his
and then I wish I hadn't.
He looks at me
and at the money
and at the fading sun
and he says,
"Drink it,
drink it probably,
and piss it all away."
He stands and walks out of
the dusty car park
the money
burning his pocket.

Rich

Billy

I stuff the notes
into my jacket pocket
and walk into town.
I think of what to do
with all this money—
a big meal at a restaurant,
some clothes,
a new sleeping bag,
a radio for the long nights,
and then I realise
how Old Bill feels—
with nothing
you're rich.
You've got no decisions,
no choice, and no worry.
Here I am walking
in the sunshine of another day
buying the world
and worrying over choices
I didn't have to make a week ago.
I want to spend the money
quickly
so I can go back to nothing,
go back to being rich
and penniless again.

Green

The thought crosses my mind
as I look at the rings
laid out on the counter
while the jeweller turns
to get some more
to show his badly-dressed customer.
But two things stop me
from stealing one silver ring
and running out of the store,
the old bloke would never
catch me, no way.
First, I want to stay
in this town,
not have to leave,
afraid of being caught.
Second, I like the jeweller.
I walked into his shop
on impulse,
smelling of overripe tomatoes
and looking far too poor
to buy anything
and here he is
showing me
his silver and gold rings
pointing out the best ones
pointing to his favourites
and letting me take my time.
And I choose
the thick silver ring

with the green emerald stone
small and shining
green like her eyes
and the jeweller says,
"$109, but let's make it
$100 cash. It's a good ring, son."
I give him the money.
He wraps it for free.

Sleep

Billy

Occasionally
I find Old Bill
asleep on the gravel
beside the carriage,
an empty bottle beside him.
I try to wake him
and help him inside
into the warmth.
He swears
and coughs
and his breath smells
of beer
and cigarettes.
We stumble into the carriage
and he falls on the seat
still swearing at me
for waking him
and at his luck for
being found
smelling badly
asleep
on the gravel
beside the train tracks
by a kid
who can't leave well enough
alone.

Need

I help Old Bill
because of Ernie
and Irene
and their friendliness.
Because when I was
twelve years old
and my dad had chased me
out of the house
with a strap,
I'd hidden in the neighbour's
chookshed, waiting for night
when I could climb
through my bedroom window
and sleep,
hoping Dad wouldn't wake angry.
After an hour,
our neighbour came out
and placed a bowl of soup
and some bread
on a tin
outside the chookshed door.
She left me dinner
and walked away.
I ate my fill
and waited till late.
A few weeks later
that neighbour moved away

and I never thanked her,
and that's why I help Old Bill,
for no reason
other than he needs it.

The mop and bucket

Caitlin

Last night
with my hated mop in one hand
and bucket in the other
I walked to Billy's table.
I stood there and he smiled,
sipped his lemonade,
and waited.
I asked him
for a date
on Saturday,
a picnic,
anywhere he wanted,
and I felt foolish
holding the mop and bucket
trying to look confident,
and he said yes
he'd love to
and I said
I'd love to as well
and I went back
to mopping
trying to act as though
nothing had happened
even though
we both knew
it had.

Caitlin

Caitlin

It's simple really.
I have more clothes
than I'll ever wear.
I have a TV and a CD player
in my room
which has its own bathroom
which is always a mess
full of make-up and lip gloss
and moisturiser and special soaps
and I have my own telephone
beside my bed.
I have a large desk with a computer
and next month,
when I turn eighteen,
my own bloody car.
And I'm not a spoilt brat OK,
but I am spoilt,
spoilt to boredom,
and I'm smart enough
to realise that none of this
means anything
except my parents are rich
and think I want this stuff
or need this stuff
and I know what I really need
and it's not in my bedroom.
And it's not able to be bought
in any damn store.

Lunchtime

Caitlin

Friday lunchtime
with Petra and Kate
under the maple tree
behind the library.
I tell them about tomorrow
and Petra giggles
and says,
"Outdoor sex, how romantic."
We all laugh,
thinking if only it were true,
then Kate
comes right out and says it,
   "I had sex once."

Grateful

Caitlin

Petra and I stare at Kate.
She doesn't look to be joking,
or proud,
or even happy.
We wait.
   "I had sex once.
   A year ago now.
   I can't tell you who with.
   And before I had sex
   I thought it would be so easy,
   so clean—that's it—
   clean and special.
   It wasn't."
I look across the schoolyard
at the Year 9s
playing netball
and two girls
arguing over a shot.
I'm afraid to look at Kate.
   "It was uncomfortable,
   it hurt,
   it was too quick
   and too messy
   and we both felt stupid.
   I closed my eyes and tried
   not to think of anything
   as he unravelled the condom
   and threw it away.
   That was it.

    Messy, quick,
    and a condom flung in the bushes.
    I had sex once
    and I've been too scared
    to have it again."
The girls at netball have stopped arguing.
They link arms
and walk into class
as the bell rings.
The three of us are quiet.
And for once
we're all grateful that
lunchtime is over.

No hurry

The knock is so quiet.
I'm not sure if she's there,
but I open the carriage door
and she says hello and
holds up a picnic basket
full of food, good food,
not takeaways,
not cold burgers,
but bread and cheese
and half a roast chicken,
and peaches, grapes, watermelon,
and a packet of Tim Tams
and a bottle opener for the beer
and on top of all the food
is the mobile phone
switched on
should her dad ring.
She's at Petra's, right.
Caitlin and I
walk to Bendarat River
and my favourite bend.
The sun is sparkling Saturday
and I've scrubbed my clothes,
at the Laundry this time
with real detergent
bought with the money I earned.
I left the ring in the carriage.
I'm in no hurry.
It's in my hiding place,

safe,
waiting for the right time
when I'm certain
it deserves a showing.
I'm in no hurry,
it's Saturday.

The picnic

Caitlin

We eat everything.
We take our time,
lying on the blanket,
a sip of beer,
a slice of cheese,
some roast,
and slowly one chocolate biscuit
after another
in the quiet sunshine—
we can't stop ourselves.
It's warm,
the food is delicious,
and the beer works its magic.
We both stretch out
on the tartan blanket
and we drift
asleep.
Our first date
Billy and me
and we sleep together
only
we really do just
sleep together
content
to waste the hours
close.

Truth and beauty
for Old Bill

I walk into the
Railway Hotel
and put $20 on the bar.
I say to the waitress,
"Keep the beer coming
until there's nothing left."
She takes the money
and replaces it with
a big cold glass
with the froth
trickling over the lip
and I think
how beautiful is a drink
that hasn't been touched,
the deep radiant colour
burning gold,
the bubbles dancing
ballet-perfect to the rim,
the sweet-bitter smell
of malt and barley.
I lift the glass
and down it
in one ignorant gulp
and I call for another
as all thoughts of
truth and beauty
wash from my mind.

Old Bill's fall

In 1993
my ten-year-old daughter Jessie
fell out of a tree
and landed bad
in a coma
in the District Hospital
and for twelve days
my wife and I
sat beside her.
I held her hand
and told stories
about our holidays together
and what she'd say to us
at dinner time or
early in the morning
when she'd climb into bed
with my wife and I.
I talked to her
so she'd remember
and wake up
and we'd go back home
as if nothing had happened.
The doctor came
with the form for us to sign
and I couldn't,
not for another four days.
I sat by Jessie
and waited.
My wife signed

and handed me the paper
and I held Jessie's hand
and signed with the other.
They switched off the machine
and Jessie lay there
for hours
still not moving,
then she died.

I went home and
took to the tree with an axe.
I was there for hours
mad with rage and pain
and God knows
that tree fell . . .

But look at me.
Kids fall out of trees
all the time.
They sprain their ankle,
or get the wind knocked out of them,
but my Jessie,
my sweet lovely Jessie,
fell
and I fell with her
and I've been falling
ever since.

And this pub,
this beer, these clothes,
this is where I landed.

The house

My wife died one year
to the day after Jessie.
She died of signing the form.
She died of making me sign
more than she died
of driving drunk
and a roadside gum tree.
After the funeral
I moved to the carriage.
I closed the door
to our house,
left everything as it was
and walked away.
The house remains
and I sometimes think
I should sell it,
or rent it,
but the thought of a family
within those walls,
people I don't know
within those walls . . .
I go there sometimes
to sit in the backyard
and remember.
I mow the grass,
then I walk back
to the Hilton

and get so drunk
I sleep for days.
I sleep, and
I don't dream.

6
Friends

*"Sure there's hope in the world
even for hobos like us."*

Comfort

Billy

Back at Wentworth High
I never talked to girls,
I hardly talked to anyone.
Sure, I answered questions from teachers
and occasionally I'd talk
to some guys I'd known for years.
But I didn't have any friends,
I didn't want any.
I had books and Westfield Creek
and I had days spent
in my bedroom reading
and avoiding my father
attached to his lounge,
his television
and his smelly unkept house.
So living in this carriage
is special, it's mine
and I keep it clean
and I read to give myself
an education that Wentworth High
never could
and I think of Caitlin
and how we fell asleep
on the picnic
so comfortable
and I don't know
what she sees in me.

I hope it's
someone to talk to
someone to look in the eye
knowing they'll look back.

Old Bill and the ghosts

Old Bill and me are friends.
Sometimes he comes into
my carriage and we share a beer.
He asks me questions
about my day
about the books I read,
he never asks me about family.
He gives me advice
on how to live cheap,
and how to jump trains
late at night,
and how to find out
which trains are going where,
and which trains have friendly Guards.
He encourages me to travel,
to leave here
and ride the Freights.
He makes it seem so special,
so romantic,
and I ask him
why he doesn't do it,
you know,
if it's so special,
and he tells me
about his Jessie
and his wife
and the house he visits
when too much drink
has made him forget

and how he's afraid to forget
because without his ghosts
he's afraid he'll have nothing to live for.
And at that moment I know
I am listening to
the saddest man in the world.

Lucky

Caitlin

No more taxi rides home
after McDonald's.
Billy walks with me.
Billy and the half-moon
and perfect stars.
We walk the long way
down Murdoch Avenue
and across the City Ovals.
The dogs bark
and each house glows
with a television light.
I tell Billy about school
and Petra, Kate,
and the drudge of exams.
Billy has become the diary entry
of my days. He holds the secrets
of every long session of Maths
and the crushing boredom
of Science on Thursday afternoon,
and as I tell him all this
I don't feel rich or poor,
or a schoolgirl, or a McDonald's worker,
or anything but lucky,
simply lucky.

Dinner

Caitlin

Dinner in our house
is always the same.
Mum's perfect cooking
and Dad's favourite wine.
He and Mum drink,
talk about work,
ask me questions about school
which I answer quickly
so as to change the subject.
Once a week
Dad brings up the topic of university
and a career for me.
His favourites are Law
and Medicine,
Mum's are Teaching and Business.
I tell them mine are Motherhood
or joining the Catholic Church
and becoming a Nun.
That shuts them up.
We eat in silence
and I think of Billy
in the carriage
waiting
for my shift to start at McDonald's.
I forget all about
careers and education
and the dreary school world.

The weekend off

Caitlin

I've got the weekend off.
No McDonald's,
no schoolwork,
and thankfully no parents—
Mum has a conference interstate,
with Dad going along
"for the golf."
It only took three days
of arguing to convince
Mum and Dad that, at seventeen,
I can be trusted on my own,
even though I can't.
And what is trust anyway?
No, I won't burn the house down.
No, I won't drink all the wine.
No, I won't have a huge drug party.
But
yes, I will invite Billy over
and yes, I will enjoy myself
in this house,
this big ugly five-bedroom
million dollar brick box
that we live in.

Hobos like us

Every morning
I wake Old Bill
with a bowl of Weet-Bix
and a cup of coffee from McDonald's,
kept hot in a Thermos overnight.
I pour us both a cup
and sit in the sunshine
as Bill groans and complains.
He sits with me and eats
and tells me how he used to be
too busy for breakfast
when he worked,
and he laughs,
a bitter, mocking laugh,
  "Too busy for breakfast,
  too busy for sitting down
  with people I loved.
  And now I've got all
  the time in the world."
But at least he eats.
And sometimes he comes with me
to Bendarat River
for a laundry and a bath.
And when he does
and he dives
fully clothed into the river
his laugh becomes real
and it's a good laugh,

a deep belly roar.
I laugh as well,
sure there's hope in the world
even for hobos like us.

The kid

Old Bill

I like the kid.
I like his company.
He's got me waking early
and eating a decent breakfast,
and yes
I drank away most of the Cannery money,
but I saved some,
just to show myself I could.
Billy and I go to the river,
we dive and swim
and wash
and for a few hours
I almost feel young again.
Billy deserves more
than an old carriage
and spending his days
trying to keep an
old hobo from too much drink.
I like the kid.

7
The simple gift

*"Wandering from room to room
discovering
another side to the moon."*

The shadows

Caitlin

I knock gently,
like I always do,
so just Billy would hear,
no-one else.
It's Friday morning
before school.
I want to tell Billy
about my parents' weekend away.
I knock again,
then I hear voices
from the next carriage
and I'm scared.
Maybe he's been discovered?
I creep around the back,
keeping to the shadows,
and I see Billy
in the carriage
with an old man
and Billy's pouring coffee
and giving it to the man
and he's pouring milk into a bowl
and handing this across
and the old man coughs
and groans and swears
and Billy sips his own coffee
and helps the old man
out of the carriage
and into the sunshine
where they sit beside the track

sharing breakfast.
And I stay in the shadows
watching
Billy and the old man
who's finished his breakfast
and Billy washes the bowl
and pours another coffee
for the old man
who is fully awake now
and the old man
looks up at Billy
and says "thanks"
and that's when I turn
and run to school
without ever leaving the shadows.

The afternoon off

Caitlin

I stop running
when I reach school
and as I enter class
I feel like a real idiot.
I sit through Maths
and Science
and English
trying to understand why I ran
and all I can think
is that seeing Billy
with that old hobo
made me think of Billy
as a hobo
and I'm ashamed,
ashamed of myself
for thinking that.
Hadn't I known
that's how Billy lived?
Hadn't I seen him
stealing food,
and hadn't I seen
where he sleeps?
By lunchtime
I decide
I'm a complete fool
and maybe I am more spoilt
than I thought,
maybe there is something
of my parents in me,

whether I like it or not.
And I walk through the school gates,
slowly and deliberately
back to the railway tracks,
determined not to run away again.

In the sunshine

Caitlin

He's in the sunshine
reading a book.
He sees me coming across the tracks
and waves,
and he stands, closes his book,
and he smiles,
and says welcome,
welcome to my sunshine,
and he jumps into the carriage,
brings out a pillow
for me to sit on.
He offers me coffee
from the same Thermos
I'd seen this morning
with the old hobo.
He keeps talking
about the book,
his favourite,
The Grapes of Wrath,
and the honour of poverty,
that's what he says,
"the honour of poverty,"
and each word he says
makes me more ashamed,
and more determined
to sit with him
here
in the bright sunshine.

A man

Caitlin

I know it was shame
that did it,
that made me do it,
but I asked Billy
and his friend, Old Bill,
to dinner at my place tonight.
I only wanted Billy
but the thought of me
running
shamed me into asking.
Billy seemed pleased
and he told me about Old Bill,
the saddest man in the world—
that's what he called him—
and as he talked
I understood
what I'd seen
this morning
and I realised
that Billy was sixteen years old
and already a man
and I was seventeen,
nearly eighteen,
and still a schoolgirl.

Cooking, and eating

Caitlin

I hate cooking.
I hate touching raw meat
and cutting it into thin slices
and peeling vegetables is boring,
so I do it all quickly.
I throw the chicken,
potatoes, beans, carrots into a pot,
I add stock,
and curry from a jar,
and I let it simmer
for hours.
I go downstairs to Dad's cellar
and choose wine,
a few bottles of red,
one white,
expensive wine
for my valued guests.
I go upstairs
and run a hot bath,
put some music on,
just quietly,
and I lie back in the full tub
and I forget cooking.
I think of eating.
I love eating.

The moon

Caitlin

I almost laugh
when they arrive.
The two neatest hobos
I've ever seen,
with their hair combed,
slicked back,
and their faces rubbed shiny clean.
Old Bill calls me "Miss"
and offers me a box of chocolates
he's brought
and he looks around the house
as though he's visiting the moon.
Billy sees the wine,
already open,
and he pours three glasses
passes them around,
and as we raise our glasses
Billy says,
"To the richest house in Bendarat"
and we laugh.
My cooking smells good
and Old Bill keeps
wandering from room to room
discovering
another side to the moon.

Stories

We can't sit at the table.
It looks too neat,
too polished, too clean.
We sit on the floor
near the fireplace
and we eat the curry
with a fork
and we dip our bread
in the sauce
and we drink just enough
to forget where we are.
Billy and I talk
and plan picnics
and nights off from McDonald's.
I tell them about school
and its stupid rules
and about Petra and Kate
and the gossip about
the two Physical Education teachers
that swept the schoolyard.
And Billy tells us about Irene
and their library deal
and reading books beside
Westfield Creek while jigging school.
Old Bill sits quiet,
a faint smile
as he slowly drinks

Dad's expensive wine
and listens
to our exaggerated
stories.

Simple gift

Old Bill

I shake the young lady's hand,
and Billy's.
I thank them for the meal
and take my leave.
I walk back
through the rich streets of town,
the neat gardens,
the high timber fences,
the solid gates with
the double garage behind them.
I haven't drunk too much,
the wine was too good to ruin
with drunkenness,
and I'd listened
to Billy and Caitlin talk
and I'd noticed
how they looked at each other—
their quick, gentle smiles over the food—
and the way they sat close,
and I realise as I walk home
that for a few hours
I hadn't thought of anything
but how pleasant it was
to sit with these people
and to talk with them.
I walk home to my old carriage
and think of how to repay them
for their simple gift,
and I enjoy the thinking.

Making love

Billy

It was like falling headlong
into the clear waters
of the Bendarat River
and opening my eyes
to the beautiful
phosphorescent bubbles of light
and trying to catch those bubbles
in the new world of quiet and calm
that carried me along, breathless,
and too late, or too early,
I surfaced
and broke the gentle tide,
and I gasped and rolled
and wished Caitlin and I
could return to the hush
of that special world
and we could float
safe for a lifetime
lost
and hoping never
to be found.

My other life

Caitlin

We fell asleep.
I fell asleep with Billy
beside me,
his arm on my stomach,
his breath so close,
and when we woke
we woke together
and he kissed me
and we made love again
in the single bed
I've had since I was eight
with its crisp white sheets
and oversized doona
and lots of pillows,
and I looked around my bedroom
at the posters on the walls
and my dresser full of make-up
and moisturiser and clutter
and my school uniform
hanging neatly behind the door
ready for my other life,
the life I'd forgotten about
for a few hours last night
and this morning.

Monday

Billy

It's early Monday.
I'm sleeping,
and I hear the knock.
I know it's not Caitlin,
her knock is quieter.
I wake with a start,
ready to run,
as the door opens
and it's Old Bill
with a coffee
and a breakfast bowl
for me.
He comes in,
sits opposite,
hands me the cup,
and he says,
"Milk and two sugars,
the way you like it.
You young blokes sure
know how to sleep,
it's 9 o'clock you know."
We look at each other
and I start laughing.
I can't help it.
I laugh long and loud,
and Old Bill,
who at first looks offended,
joins in,
two hobos laughing,
laughing the morning away.

117

Tell the world

Caitlin

On Monday at school
I sit with Petra and Kate
and I want to tell
them about everything.
I so much want to tell
but I can't
because
of Kate
and her story
of sex in the bushes
and I don't want
to have to talk about
the details
as if to prove to her
that it was good
and fine
and I feel lucky
and I don't want to admit
that I can't wait to see Billy
and do it again
and again
and that somehow
while mopping the floor
at McDonald's
I'd met someone
who I could lie naked beside
and not feel foolish
or embarrassed,
that I'd met someone

I can trust
and feel safe with.
I want to tell them that,
but not yet,
not just yet.
I want to go to Billy
tonight
and tomorrow
and next week
and I want to prove it
to myself
before I tell the world.

Share

Caitlin

Sometimes
before my McDonald's shift,
I pack my bag
with food—
bread, cheese,
some fruit—
for Billy.
Enough for Billy
but not enough
for my parents
to get suspicious.
At first
Billy said, "No, no way,"
but I reminded him
of our house,
"the richest house in Bendarat,"
he'd said.
He takes the food,
promising to share it
with Old Bill.

Billy, dancing

I spend $5 on candles,
two dozen candles,
and I work all day
looking for tins
and scraps of metal
and discarded old mugs,
anything to stand a candle in.
As evening comes
I light each candle
let the wax drop onto the tin
and stand the candle
firm in its wax,
and soon enough
I have twenty-four candles
burning in my carriage
and each throws a dancing shadow
on the walls
and the windows covered
with cardboard.
I shake my sleeping bag
and spread it neatly
across the bench seat
and I sweep the floor
and push my bag
under the seat
and I wait for Caitlin
to walk into
the brilliant soft light
of twenty-four candles
dancing for her.

Heaven

Caitlin

It's like stepping
into heaven,
all that light,
with Billy smiling
on the seat,
proud of what he's created.
As I step
into the carriage
I close the door
to everything,
and I go to Billy
as if we've been
doing this for years
and the candles
burn long and gentle
as we lay together
for hours.
What can I say?
It's like stepping
into heaven,
no less than perfect.

The clink of the bottles

Old Bill

I see Billy
kissing his girl Caitlin
on the train tracks
as they walk off.
Billy returns an hour later
and comes to my carriage.
We sit opposite, talking.
I hear the bottles clink
in his bag
and I say,
"Come on then,
let's have them."
But when he brings out
the ginger beer
I swear
and laugh
and swear some more,
but really
you've got to admire the kid.
So I drink the stuff
and we sit up late
talking
and I sleep
better than I have in a long time
so maybe
just maybe
I'll work on less beer
for a while.
For the kid's sake.

8
Closing in

*"I try to read
between the lines
holding someone's past
in my dirty hands."*

Old Bill and this town

I wake early,
I eat properly,
for breakfast at least,
and I've taken to walking
every day.
I go to the river with Billy
and we swim and wash,
or sometimes
I walk the streets
looking at the houses
and the corner shops
and the parks with trees
and fountains,
and young couples kissing,
and old men reading newspapers,
and ladies walking dogs,
and sometimes
these people nod and say hello
as though I'm one of them
and not an old drunk.
I nod back,
even talk about the weather on occasions,
and I walk back to my carriage
planning
where I'll go tomorrow,
where I'll walk in my town
where I'll go to stop
thinking about the drink.

Nothing's easy

Old Bill

"Nothing's easy."
That's what Billy says
when I tell him about my walks
and how I pass a pub
and my hands start shaking
and it would only take
a few steps
to be at the bar
ordering a pint . . .

And the young kid,
sharp as a tack,
says,
"Don't walk near a pub then."
We look at each other
and I say,
"Nothing's easy."

Bloody cops.
I hate to lie.
I hate it,
but with two of them
on Main Street
asking me questions,
questions I can't answer
honestly,
I make up what I can.
I say I'm passing through,
I'm staying with a friend,
I've been working at the Cannery
and now I'm heading west.
I'm eighteen,
old enough to look after myself.
They don't believe a word,
I can tell,
but I haven't done anything wrong,
and the older cop,
he's smart,
he knows what to do.
He gives me a card,
> *Department of Community Services*
> *Welfare Officer: Brent Stevens*
He says he'll meet me
at the office tomorrow
at 4 P.M.
and if I don't show
well, fine, I've moved on,

128

but if he sees me
in town again
and I haven't shown,
he'll ask more questions,
and this time
he'll want some answers.
Bloody cops.
Bloody welfare.

I walk home
to the Bendarat Hilton
and I lay in bed
with the old carriage walls
closing in.

Old Bill's long walk

Old Bill

Today
I walk past
Jessie's old school.
It's had a paint job,
and they've built a new library.
It's lunchtime
and the children are outside.
The big kids are
playing cricket on the oval.
The young children
play in the sandpit.
A few girls are sitting
and talking under a tree.
As I walk by
one of the girls
starts to climb the tree.
I'm about to say something
when a young teacher
comes over:
"Sarah, no climbing trees."
The teacher smiles at me
and walks back to
the shade of the school veranda.
I can feel my hands
shaking
as I walk back to town.
I walk the long way,
careful not to go past a pub.

Early, or late   Billy

I wake early,
go to Old Bill's carriage
with coffee and breakfast
and he's already awake,
he's shaving!
We sit in the sunshine
and I tell him
about the cops
and ask what I should do?
I know Welfare will ask
about where I live
and how I live
and I have to keep them
as far away from here
as I can
and it seems that
moving out west
is the only answer.
But how can I leave
the only town
I've ever wanted to call home,
and Caitlin . . .

Home

When young Billy
tells me about the cops
I know I have to do something.
I tell him not to worry,
that somehow
we'll come up with an idea.
I leave Billy to his coffee
and his fears of leaving town.
I want a long walk to think.
I avoid the park—
today I don't need conversation,
I need time.
I walk the suburbs
looking at the neat lawns,
the pebbled driveways,
the flowers and hedges,
and the paint jobs of
a thousand everyday dreams.
And I think of Billy
leaning against the carriage
reading a book
waiting,
as I walk
the familiar streets
of Bendarat.

So obvious

Old Bill

I walk for hours
to end up here
in Wellington Road
opposite
my house,
Jessie's house.
I sit on a bus seat
looking across,
picturing Jessie
at the window
in the backyard
on the veranda.
I could use a drink
to help me decide
but
I know Billy has only got
until this afternoon
and I know
that what I must do is
so obvious
and simple
and so unbearably painful
my whole body shakes
with the thought.

To help people

Old Bill

Sitting here
I thought of Jessie
and the injured bird.
Jessie was eight years old,
she found a parrot
unable to move.
We placed it in a shoe-box
wrapped in a hand-towel
to keep warm,
hoping the shock would subside.
Jessie stroked its head,
she prayed,
she fed it sugar syrup
with an eye dropper
and we stayed up late,
waiting.
It took two days
of Jessie praying
and stroking
and feeding,
and the bird got stronger.
Jessie and I stood on the veranda,
Jessie holding the bird gently.
She opened her hands
and it sat on her palms
looking at her
then it turned and flew
high into the wattle
where it perched.

Jessie waved
and the bird flew away.

I thought of Jessie
helping that bird
and how, after it left,
Jessie turned to me
and said that
when she grew up
she wanted to be a vet,
she wanted to heal animals
and to help people.

Peace

Old Bill

I unlatch the gate to my house
and walk around the backyard,
the wattle is in bloom,
and a pair of swallows
have made a nest
of clay and straw
under the veranda ceiling.
It's so quiet,
the grass is knee-high
and I think of the lawnmower
in the shed.
I'm sure I can find some two-stroke
and with a bit of coaxing
get the thing started,
but for now
I sit on the veranda
and admire the peace
that I'd never noticed here,
with the morning sun
filtering through the trees,
and I understand
why it's so quiet,
so unworldly.
The swallows swoop along
the grass and weeds
and arc into the nest
above my head.
I hear the chirp of
young birds after a feed

and I stand, walk to the shed,
unlock the door,
push the cobwebs away,
and I roll out the old mower
and go rummaging
for some two-stroke,
ready to work.

The neighbours

Old Bill

The house next door
has new owners
and when they see me
mowing
they come to the fence
to ask questions,
so many questions.
I tell them
I own this house
but live elsewhere
and I've just rented it out
to a young lad,
a friend of the family,
and he's moving in soon
and he'll keep this grass mown
and look after the place
for me,
an old man
with a house
too big for him.
That seems to please them,
they stop asking questions
and talk about
the weather instead.
I go back to mowing.
I'm no good with neighbours
and I wonder if
I ever will be.

War

Today in History
in Room 652
I look out the window
and see Billy
sitting across the road
with his head in his hands.
I want to rush out
cross the road
and hug him
right there in the park
opposite my school
and we can walk
to his carriage
and make love
while Petra and Kate
and the rest of this class
learn about the Vietnam War.
Billy and I can make love
not war
and Billy looks so sad.
I want so much
to flee History
and the murderous armies
and Mr Hawkins
handing out
homework sheets
that give me more work
to keep me away from
Billy and freedom

x

and I feel like
a prisoner of war
here in Room 652
while Billy
sits in the park
with his head in his hands.

Not moving

All morning
I sit outside Bendarat Grammar
hoping to see Caitlin,
wishing she'd walk through
those big iron gates
and we could run away
from Bendarat
and cops
and nosy Welfare officers
who call you by your first name
after every sentence,
    "So where are you living, Billy?"
    "Do you have enough food, Billy?"
    "Do you want to go back to school,
Billy?"
    "I'm only here to help, Billy."
All morning
I sit in the dull sunshine
waiting for something to happen.
I think about Old Bill
and what he said.
I guess he's going to
give me the last of his money
from the Cannery work,
and a map of Australia,
and tell me which train
to jump on to get out of town
before 4 P.M. like I'm some dangerous cowboy
being run out of town by the Sheriff.

All morning
I think of Caitlin
and I think of leaving
and
all morning
I sit opposite the school
not moving,
not moving a muscle.

Old Bill's suit and tie

Old Bill

Before meeting Billy
I go to the Salvation Army shop.
I buy a clean shirt
and trousers
and a tie.
I pack my old clothes
in a plastic bag
and walk out
a businessman
ready to impress the world.

Everything takes longer
than I expect,
mowing the grass,
buying clothes,
paying the electricity deposit,
so I walk quickly,
with my plan getting clearer,
sure I'm doing
the only thing I can,
sure it's right
because
it's the only way
for him to stay in Bendarat
near Caitlin.
I'm exhausted
when I turn the corner
and see Billy
sitting against a wall
with his backpack
and his troubled grin,
but
when I see him
I feel something
I haven't felt in
many years.
I feel pride.

All that knowledge

Old Bill

I wasn't always a hobo.
I worked in town.
I dressed neatly in suit and tie.
I understood the Law.
I earned a lot of money
knowing stupid rules and regulations
and I'd studied for years
to make sure those rules
were enforced
when someone came to me for help.
But all that knowledge
and all that training
couldn't stop a young
beautiful child from
falling out of a tree,
or a wife from driving
a car too drunk to care.
All that knowledge
couldn't stop a man
from drinking to forget
to forget the life
with the suit and tie
in his office in town.
But today
the knowledge
that hasn't been used
in five years
can come up
with a solution

to where a sixteen-year-old boy
can live,
and what his legal rights are,
so all that knowledge
is finally worth something,
finally.

Old and young

I tell Billy
I want to buy him a coffee
to pay him back,
you know,
for every morning coffee
and breakfast.
He doesn't want to come.
He wants to see Caitlin
and tell her his problem.
I tell Billy
to sit, and enjoy his coffee,
as the waitress brings
two cups of steaming brew.
Billy looks out the window
and I see the first signs of defeat
in his young eyes.
I know how it looks,
and I know, right then,
I've made the right decision
and I tell him
my plan
without stopping,
my plan.

Old Bill's plan

It's so simple.
Billy lives in Wellington Road, alone.
We'll tell the Welfare I live there too.
I'm a family friend helping Billy out.
We'll talk about
the drunken dangerous angry father.
Billy looking for work
or considering returning to school.
Welfare people like that talk.
We'll mention our work at the Cannery.
We'll talk about how I can help Billy
with the cost of living in such a big home.
We'll talk non-stop.
We won't let Welfare talk
their welfare bullshit.
We'll say everything's taken care of
and we'll prove it.
And we'll leave that office,
go straight to Wellington Road
and let Billy start his new life
in a house that needs a new life,
happier than the old one.

Billy

Billy

I hold the keys
to Wellington Road
as Old Bill talks
and tries to convince me
and himself
that we can fool the
Welfare worker and the cops.
I listen to Old Bill
and know we can do it
but
as I listen
I know that I'll never
never in my life
feel sadder
than I do right now
because
I know
that Old Bill is giving me
more than these keys I hold.
And as I hold these keys
I'm not sure
if taking them
means Old Bill
has a new life too
or if taking them means
he now has nothing,
nothing at all to hold.
I clutch the keys
and I listen to Old Bill

and I try to read
between the lines
holding someone's past
in my dirty hands.

Caitlin

Caitlin

I rush out of school
but Billy has gone
so I go to his carriage
and knock.
He isn't here
and I think of him
outside school
looking so lonely.
I know something is wrong.
I walk home
making plans
to finish at McDonald's
tonight
and return to his carriage
with two apple pies
and some coffee,
eager to listen.

Liars

Luckily
the old cop didn't stay.
He introduced Old Bill and me
to Brent Stevens, the Welfare worker
who took us into his office
and asked us lots of questions,
"Billy this, Billy that."
And Old Bill
told him our story,
and I've got to admit
Old Bill is one hell of a good liar!
When I asked him later
how he lied so well,
he laughed aloud,
and said he used to do it for a living.
I don't know if Mr Stevens
believed us or not,
but I knew
he couldn't do a thing about it.
I was sixteen.
I was living with a responsible adult
in a normal house,
and I planned to go back to school.
All lies,
but believable lies.
We shook hands with Mr Stevens
and he wished me luck

when I knew
I had so much already.
Old Bill and I walked out
into bright afternoon sunshine.

9
Locks and keys

"We shake,
and my hand in his
stops trembling
for a moment."

I hug Old Bill
like I've never hugged
a man before
sure that he's saved my life.
I hug him in Main Street
with the office workers walking by,
and the shopkeepers staring,
and the two old ladies at the bus stop
watching the big grey-haired man
wrap his arms around the teenager
and I thank him once
and thank him a hundred times.
I shoulder the rucksack
and we walk up the hill
to the better part of town
with the neat gardens
and orderly trees
and brightly coloured fences
to Wellington Road
with the freshly mown grass
and the swallows
celebrating a birth
in the nest
above the veranda.

Swallows

Billy

Old Bill and I
sit on the veranda
watching the swallows
swoop and play
with a gentle breeze blowing
through the fir trees
along the back fence.
Old Bill tells me
he planted those trees
their first year here
and he built the shed himself
and this veranda used to have
a gas BBQ for summer evenings,
sipping wine and cooking steak,
and they had a dog,
Jerry,
a little cockerspaniel
who loved sausages,
who'd leap in the air
when Old Bill threw her a snag.
Old Bill tells me they
lived here for fifteen years
and he closed the door
and locked it on March 2nd, 1994.
He tells me he comes back
occasionally,
"To sit on the veranda
and cry, like an old drunk."
I hold the key in my hands.

I know better than to ask him inside.
I know he hasn't been inside
since that March day,
and I'm not going to force the issue,
not for my sake.
I pocket the key,
say thanks, again,
and we both walk back to town.
I'm not going inside
without Caitlin with me.
I can wait.

Tremor

Old Bill

My hands still shake
from the drink
or lack of it
so when I can
I walk with them
deep in my pockets
so people won't see
my tremors.
Billy and I sit on the veranda
and I tell him
about the BBQ
and Jerry
and her acrobatic tricks.
I keep my hands
in my pockets.
Billy holds the key,
returns it to his pocket,
says thanks, again,
and offers his strong young hand.
We shake,
and my hand in his
stops trembling
for a moment.

Locks and keys

Billy

It's been too long
since I've seen Caitlin
and I say sorry
as soon as I walk
into McDonald's
and she smiles
even though she's mopping!
I order a lemonade
and sit upstairs.
I've got so much to tell her
and I don't know how.
A house seems so . . .
so . . .
so adult,
even though
it's only for a short time
until the Welfare
are off my track
and I can decide
what I really want to do
here in Bendarat.

Caitlin and the key

Caitlin

Billy told me last night
to meet him here
on the corner of Wellington and Jamison
after school.
I feel very silly
here on the footpath
in my school uniform
with an umbrella
as the rain tumbles down.
And Billy walks towards me,
wet and grinning like a madman.
We kiss, and he takes my hand
and leads me down Wellington Road,
a long way from his train carriage.
I ask question after question
but I can tell
it's a surprise
and he doesn't want to tell me,
he wants to show me.
So I hold my impatience
and he leads me
into the driveway
of a beautiful white timber house
with an old shed
and a huge backyard
of trees—wattles and firs—
and one of those homemade bird feeders
on a pole near the fence,
and there's a King Parrot

sitting, eating some seed.
Billy and I stand on the veranda.
He hands me a key
and we stand, his hand on mine,
the key between us,
and he tells me
about the cops and Welfare
and Old Bill's story
and Old Bill's plan
and how they both
sat on the veranda yesterday
talking
rather than taking the key
this key I hold
and turning it in the lock.
And Billy looks at me,
he wants me to do it with him,
because of this house
and its past
and what it means to Old Bill.
It's all too much.
I start to cry
because I think of Old Bill
and what I thought
when I first saw him
swearing and waiting for breakfast
from Billy
and I think of both of them
at dinner at my house

with their hair neat
and the three of us
sitting on the floor to eat.
I feel the tears
and I turn towards the door,
I insert the key
and turn it slowly
and push the door.
I reach behind for Billy's hand
and we walk inside.

10
Old Bill

*"The swallows
sing on the veranda,
as Caitlin and I
stand here
measuring a life."*

Old Bill

Old Bill

Tonight, in my carriage,
I remember telling Billy ages ago
to travel,
to jump some Freights
and see the country.
I thought it crazy,
a young bloke living like a bum
here in Bendarat,
in an old train carriage.
But Billy stayed
and we worked at the Cannery
and he kept waking me
with breakfast
and often
we'd spend nights
sitting in the dark, talking,
and those nights
were the nights I stopped drinking.
I had something better to do.
And tonight
I think of Billy
and Caitlin
in the house together
and I'm still not drinking.
I'm thinking of an old hobo,
months ago,
offering advice to a young kid

when he should have been listening
to his own words
ringing
hollow in his head.

A project

When Jessie was nine
she did a school project
on the Great Barrier Reef.
Together we hunted for books
on fish and sealife and the rainforests
and Jessie loved cutting the pictures
from magazines and pasting them
onto a huge cardboard sheet.
She wanted to learn to dive
among the fish in the warm
tropical waters thousands of miles away.
We kept cutting and pasting
and I promised her we'd go
and I promised her we'd swim together
and wave at the fish!
The Great Barrier Reef.
Queensland,
where they have work
for fruit pickers
watermelons,
pineapples,
bananas.
I could do that.
I could hop the Freights
all the way north
where it's warm.
I could stay for winter
and I could be sure
that Billy was looking after

everything I own,
for when I get back
from taking Jessie's
trip to the ocean.

Measure

Billy

Caitlin and I walk
through the house,
brushing the spiderwebs
from the doorways,
treading carefully,
quiet, like in a museum.
The furniture is old
but solid.
There's a television,
and a stereo
with lots of country records
stacked neatly beside.
The curtains
are beautiful,
white cotton with seashell patterns
in vivid blue,
and in the bedroom
the wardrobes are solid old timber,
empty,
the double bed is neatly made,
and the dresser is clear
of photos, or books, or anything personal.
The kitchen is huge
with a big fridge,
a double sink,
lots of bench space,
a place where someone
had enjoyed cooking.
Caitlin and I walk around

touching everything gently
as though each object
is worth a fortune.
At the entrance
to the smaller bedroom
we find some pencil marks
on the wall,
we lean in to read them—
—Jessie 1.2.91
—Dad 1.2.91
—Mum 14.6.92
—Jessie 14.6.92
—Dad 1.2.93
—Jessie 1.2.93.
Under the last entry
for Jessie
in a child's printing
are the words
"I've grown 13 centimetres in 2 years,
lots more than Dad!"
The swallows
sing on the veranda,
as Caitlin and I
stand here
measuring a life.

Cleaning

Caitlin

I tell Mum and Dad
the truth.
Well, some of it is true.
I tell them
I'm helping a friend
clean their house
and that's why
I've got the mop,
yes, the hated mop,
and a bucket,
and lots of rags.
And I tell them
I'll be away all day
and I leave quickly
before they can ask me
what friend, and where?
I arrive at Billy's
and he's in the kitchen
scrubbing the floor.
He's already done the bathroom.
I vacuum the lounge
and the main bedroom—
it's only dust
that's gathered lonely in the corners
and on the curtains.
Billy and I work all morning.
We eat lunch under the fir trees
and look at the house.
We don't say much.

We lie on the blanket
and hold each other.
Billy has his arms around me
and his eyes turned
towards the white timber house.

Saturday dinner

Caitlin

I ring Mum on the mobile
and I tell her I'll be late home.
I'm having dinner at my friend's.
She starts to ask who
and I switch the mobile off,
deliberately.
I'm having dinner at Billy's,
a dinner we will cook together,
and afterwards
we'll make love on the bed,
Billy's bed.
Then we'll get dressed
and Billy will walk home with me,
and I'll walk into Mum and Dad's questions,
and I'll answer them
truthfully.
It's time.
I love Billy, and I'm sure of him.
I want my parents to know.
In two weeks I'll be eighteen
and I want my parents to know
what I do,
what I plan to do.
I put the mobile down
on the kitchen bench
and I help Billy prepare
the Saturday dinner.

The best meal

Billy

It is the best meal
I've ever eaten.
Chicken curry,
with rice and cashew nuts
and pappadums.
It takes Caitlin and me
all afternoon to prepare.
We kept stopping to put on
another of Old Bill's records.
We slow-danced around the lounge
to wailing country music,
laughing at our foolish steps
and holding each other
to stop from falling,
and Caitlin tries to lead
and I try to lead
and we both give up
and go back to the curry.
We each pour a beer
and sit at the dinner table
with a white tablecloth
and napkins
and proper cutlery and plates.
I raise my glass,
Caitlin does the same
and we both say,
"To Old Bill,"
and we drink

and we each eat two helpings
of curry and rice.
It is the best meal
I've ever eaten.

Value

Billy

Caitlin and I lay
in the huge bed
with the moon
a perfect light
and the trees
long fingers scratching
at the window.
I reach under the bed
and find what I'd hidden
earlier in the night.
I lift the small case
and I open the lid
to show Caitlin the
beautiful green emerald ring
I'd bought months earlier
because of the colour of her eyes
because I'd worked all week
in the Cannery with my hands stained red
and because
I couldn't spend all that money
on food,
or beer,
or myself.

11
The hobo sky

"The taste of being sober
all day."

Midnight

Billy

Last night,
unable to sleep
in this quiet house
without the freight train whistles
and the diesel shunting back and forth,
I got dressed, closed the door gently,
and walked the streets,
and as the Town Hall clock
tolled midnight
I stood on the railway platform
looking across at the carriages,
my home for these past months.
I knew Old Bill was asleep
like most of Bendarat.
I made a silent vow
to visit my carriage,
once a week,
to sit and read, alone, on the leather seat,
with the sounds and smells
of the hobo life close by,
to never forget this home
by the railroad tracks.

Drinking by the river

Billy

Today
Old Bill and I meet at the river.
I bring some lunch
and soft drinks.
Old Bill laughs
when I pass him a ginger beer.
We sit by the bank
watching the sun sparkle
on the water,
with the ducks gliding by
and an ibis on the opposite bank
near a log
looking for food,
as Old Bill
tells me about his job
years ago
in an office
with his name on the door
and the days he worked overtime
not getting home
until late
with his wife waiting
and Jessie in bed
reading a book
determined not to fall asleep
until he arrived home.
We watch the ibis
search under the log.
Old Bill tells me about

the Trust Account
from those days,
that pays him just enough.
He drinks his ginger beer
and pulls a face at its sweetness.
He sees me watching him
and says
it's taking a while
for him to get used to
the taste of being sober
all day.

Respect   *Billy*

It feels strange
sleeping in a bed again
with sheets crisp and clean
and a big doona,
and being able to watch television
and play music
and cook the proper food
that Caitlin brings.
I wander through the house,
so big,
much bigger than a train carriage.
I love the curtains,
yes, I know it's weird,
but I love closing the world out
by pulling them across
and in the morning
spreading them wide
and letting the sunshine through.
It feels like a home
where I can look out
and not be afraid of who sees me,
or who I see.
Every morning
I clean this house
and I don't let anything break
or get dirty
because this house
is not mine.
I know I'm only here

for a while
so I tread lightly
with respect
for this house
and for Old Bill.

Maybe

Billy

I tell Irene
about my new house
and Old Bill.
She says she's glad
but worried
about money for me
living in the house.
I think about the Cannery
and fruit-picking.
Irene goes over to the Resource section,
brings back a TAFE Handbook
and an application form
for government study assistance.
If they paid me
maybe,
just maybe,
I'd go back to school.

I take the form and the book,
tell Irene I'll think about it,
and maybe
I will.

Holiday

I wake early, at sunrise.
I fill the Thermos with
steaming hot strong coffee.
I pack Weet-Bix and milk
into my rucksack
and I walk the quiet dawn streets
to Bendarat Freight Yard.
I knock gently, twice,
and open Old Bill's door
to the sound of his snoring.
I pour the coffee
and he wakes, swearing as usual,
with me laughing
that anyone could wake so angry.
Old Bill swears some more
then laughs at himself
as he starts breakfast.
Today he eats three helpings
and drinks the Thermos
and on his last cup
he tells me of his plan
to head north, taking his time.
And he says,
"Don't worry about the house
and its ghosts,
I'm taking them with me,
they need a holiday,
and so do I."
I don't know what to say,

so I sit here
looking at the freight train
shunting carriages in the distance
across the tracks
where
months ago
an old man
dropped his beer
and sat down to cry.
I say to Old Bill,
"I love the house,"
and I leave it at that.

The hobo sky

Billy

After breakfast
I clean the bowls
and pack everything
back into my rucksack.
We shake hands
and I tell him
the Bendarat Hilton
is the best motel
I've ever stayed in.
Old Bill laughs
and says, "Me too."
I cross the tracks
heading to the library.
When I look back
I see Old Bill
with his back to me
looking up at the sky.
He stands there for a long time,
not moving,
like he's praying,
then he picks up his swag
and walks slowly,
deliberately,
north.
I watch until he
is out of sight
and I look up
into the sky,
the deep blue sky
that Old Bill and I share.